CU00900792

This book belongs to

_____

_____

Look out for other Piccolo and Annabelle books:

A Very Messy Inspection
The Stinky Cheese Gypsies

Piccolo and Annabelle

VOLUME TWO

A DISASTROUS

PARTY

WRITTEN AND ILLUSTRATED BY

STEPHEN AXELSEN

OXFORD
UNIVERSITY PRESS

OXFORD
UNIVERSITY PRESS

Great Clarendon Street, Oxford OX2 6DP

Oxford University Press is a department of the University of Oxford.
It furthers the University's objective of excellence in research, scholarship,
and education by publishing worldwide in

Oxford   New York

Auckland   Cape Town   Dar es Salaam   Hong Kong   Karachi
Kuala Lumpur   Madrid   Melbourne   Mexico City   Nairobi
New Delhi   Shanghai   Taipei   Toronto

With offices in

Argentina   Austria   Brazil   Chile   Czech Republic   France   Greece
Guatemala   Hungary   Italy   Japan   Poland   Portugal   Singapore
South Korea   Switzerland   Thailand   Turkey   Ukraine   Vietnam

Oxford is a registered trade mark of Oxford University Press
in the UK and in certain other countries

First published in 2005 by Random House Australia Pty Ltd, Sydney, Australia.
This edition published by arrangement with Random House Australia.
First published in the UK in 2006

British Library Cataloguing in Publication Data

Data available

ISBN-13: 978-0-19-272610-0
ISBN-10: 0-19-272610-2

1 3 5 7 9 10 8 6 4 2

Printed and bound by Mackays of Chatham plc, Chatham, Kent

For my lovely Lauren Rose

CONTENTS

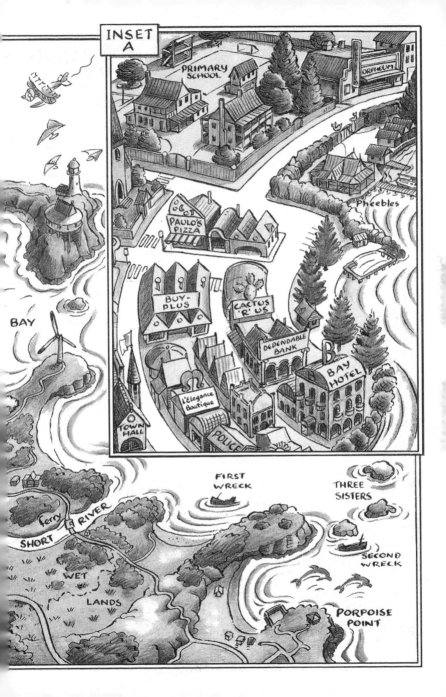

Holywell, No. 9 Pleasant Crescent

CHAPTER ONE
Mr Yow

He's watching me, thought Piccolo. He's been watching me all day. Piccolo could feel eyes boring into the top of his head. He was trying to concentrate on covering a library book, a special talent of his. No one could put self-adhesive plastic on a library book the way Piccolo Grande could. Except for today.

'Oh no, a wrinkle,' he moaned. He looked up quickly and yelped. Those bushy black eyebrows were there again, bristling above the window sill. The same eyebrows had been following him since he arrived at school that day, peeking around corners, through bushes, over rows of bins, and now through the library window. They were the eyebrows of Mr Yow, the new groundsman, a strange looking fellow with very long arms and a waddling walk, and enough hair to stuff a mattress.

'Creepy, sneaky creep,' Piccolo muttered as he snapped the blind shut.

'Not talking about me, I hope,' said a voice behind him. Piccolo yelped again. Today was too full of surprises.

It was Stella McKellar. 'Are you OK, Piccolo Grande? You look jumpy. And—oh dear—you've wrinkled that cover.'

'I'm fine,' blushed Piccolo. He tried to peel back the plastic to restick it, but tore the cover. If Stella did one thing well and easily it was make Piccolo blush. She was in the year ahead of him at school and twenty centimetres taller. Piccolo thought she was the prettiest girl in the

known universe, and could *not* understand why she would even talk to him. Unless she just enjoyed watching him turn pink, then red, then crimson. He was burgundy—a deep purple crimson—now.

'Something's wrong. You've torn the cover. Is it Mr Yow?'

Piccolo spun around to look at her properly.

'Creepy, isn't he, and constantly scratching. I hope he doesn't give us fleas,' she said. 'I've been watching him watching you. You're nice enough, but you're not *that* interesting.'

Did Stella just say I was *nice?* thought the burgundy boy, with a lurching tummy. The last bell of the day rang.

'See you tomorrow, Piccolo,' sang Stella as she left the library.

'Yes. Good,' said Piccolo.

She called me *nice*, thought Piccolo more than once as he walked home. He stopped at a crossing and was repeating this happy thought for the ninth time when he felt eyes upon him again. He looked behind, expecting to see Mr Yow ducking behind a parked car. But there was nothing unusual; just the usual bluey-green uniforms of Clearwater Bay Public School, and a mother or two. The lollipop lady waved them across the road. She was a new lollipop lady, with one long hairy arm holding her sign, and another scratching her head. Heavy eyebrows and beetly black

4

eyes followed Piccolo to the other side.

Creepy and creepier, thought Piccolo as he hurried home.

'Annabelle, I think I'm being watched.'

Piccolo's Great-Aunt Annabelle was busy at the kitchen table shuffling through a small mountain of letters and labels from baked bean tins.

'That's nice, dear,' she said, smiling but absent.

'Yes, crocodiles are watching me with miniature telescopes,' he tried again.

'Oh excellent, dear. I always knew you would one day. Have you seen the scissors?'

Piccolo sighed. 'They're behind your ear.' This was true. His great-aunt's hair was tough and wild and useful for storing small objects.

'So they are, my brilliant detective. You want me to watch you do what?'

'Never mind,' said Piccolo and he trudged upstairs to his room. Some guardian angel she is, he thought grumpily.

Piccolo's Great-Aunt Annabelle was not really his aunt, or any kind of relative at all. She was in fact his own personal guardian angel sent by higher angels to look after him. But she had been a distracted angel lately. She was busy as a buck-toothed beaver entering and winning competitions, lotteries, and raffles of all shapes and kinds.

Piccolo dropped his bag in a corner, neatly, and flopped on his bed, tidily. He tried to empty his mind, but bushy eyebrows and beetly black eyes kept appearing in there.

'Stamps!' he said aloud. From his stamp cupboard he chose an album and sat at his desk.

'Ah! Eastern European, 1910 to 1925,' he sighed happily, and began to flip through the pages. After a few minutes he sighed *un*happily. The stamps were not cheering him up. In fact, they were boring.

'It's all her fault. She's muddled up my tidy life completely.' He stared hard through the floor in Annabelle's direction. 'I need to bounce.'

So he bounced. Up and over and down and over, inside out and around and down, on a trampoline Annabelle had won in a raffle. They had put it in the ballroom to help Annabelle keep up her flying fitness. Up and twist and double somersault. Piccolo was getting very good. Annabelle hummed tunelessly across the hall in the kitchen, as she snipped and stuck and stacked things.

Piccolo muttered to himself as he bounced. 'Everything'—flip— 'used to be'—twist—'so calm and quiet'—bounce—'before she came'— flip twist—'but now it's all chaos and . . .'

'AAAAGH,' screamed Annabelle.

Piccolo twisted when he should have flipped and landed badly on the edge of the trampoline.

Annabelle burst into the ballroom. 'Piccolo! I've won! I've won!' she bellowed joyously.

'You . . . always . . . win,' said Piccolo, doubled over and breathing heavily.

'Yes, but this time it was *skill*, not dumb luck!

'I've won! I've won!' she bellowed joyously.

Are you all right, dear?'

'I'll be fine,' he wheezed, wondering if he'd broken a rib or two. 'What did you win?'

'Remember my Party People jingle?

If you're ninety-eight and shaky,
or if you're just sixteen and flaky,
be you glum or hale and hearty,
it's always time to throw a party!

We've won a party, Piccolo!'

Piccolo smiled weakly, but he was not happy. A party person he was not. Annabelle most definitely was. She skipped about with excitement.

'We can have it anywhere, any time! They provide food and tents and costumes and rides— even stamps and envelopes for invitations! We'll invite everyone! Here! We'll have it here, yes?'

'Or how about on the dark side of the moon?' said Piccolo, but his guardian angel was not listening and missed his gloomy suggestion.

'We'll celebrate us, you and me, living happy as geese in a tree!' she trilled, and chatted on rapidly about the great joys to come, for one and all, and others as well.

Oh, dear. We're having a party, thought Piccolo miserably. So very, very many things could go wrong.

CHAPTER TWO
Party Planning

'Lists! Parties need lists. You are an excellent list-maker, Piccolo.'

Annabelle knew that he could never resist a list. List-making always improved his mood.

She swept away her labels and magazines, forms and entries, off the kitchen table onto the floor. Piccolo looked at the great mess and sighed.

'Now, all your friends will come. Write down their names here, Piccolo,' said Annabelle, and she slapped down a two-hundred-page pad in front of him, and one for herself.

Piccolo carefully sharpened his pencil. Annabelle found a bottle of ink, then reaching behind herself she yanked hard, plucking a feather from her wing.

'Doesn't that hurt?' asked Piccolo, as Annabelle sharpened the feather with a penknife to make a pen.

'Oh, not much,' she said, already dipping and scribbling names. 'Angels are tough. You'll sharpen that pencil to death, Piccolo. It's list time, my boy!'

Piccolo did not have a lot of friends, not two hundred pages' worth; more like two lines' worth. Since his dear parents had vanished he'd kept mostly to himself.

But maybe, just maybe, Stella will come, he thought.

He carefully wrote 'Stella McKellar' and a question mark, and without thinking he wrote 'xxx'. Blushing, he quickly rubbed them out. The list-making stalled.

'How's it coming along?' asked Annabelle, on her second page already. Hers was becoming a fulsome list. Nearly everybody in Clearwater Bay was on it, including mad Mrs Lin who lived out of a shopping trolley and the scruffy dog who lived at the bus stop.

Piccolo stood at her shoulder watching Annabelle's list grow.

'I don't think the Prime Minister will come, Annabelle. He's very busy.'

'You never know. Even PMs need a party!' and she sang her jingle again.

She called out a lot of unusual names as she jotted them down: Ezekial Fulbright, Raziel Lovejoy . . .

'Gabriel Gladheart, and these others . . . are you inviting angels, Annabelle?'

'I'm not allowed to say, dear.'

'You're inviting Mr Purvis? He's an angel, although not a very nice one.'

'Oh, he is probably very nice . . . deep inside, dear. And it would be rude not to ask him along. He did pass me on my Inspection, after all.'

Mr Purvis, Pest Exterminator, was the local Inspector of Guardian Angels, in disguise. He was a stern and humourless little angel with a nasty trimmed moustache. Piccolo remembered the terrible day of the Inspection.

'Don't forget to be careful around him if he

comes. He must not guess that you are an Angelspotter,' Annabelle reminded him.

'Oh yes. I'm an *Angelspotter*,' said Piccolo rolling his eyes. 'The special kind of non-angelspotting Angelspotter.' Piccolo had serious doubts that he was such a thing.

According to Annabelle a genuine Angelspotter could spot an angel by its golden glow. Piccolo had never seen a golden glow, not even around his own personal live-in guardian angel; just a halo of wild red hair.

'You'll get the knack soon enough, my love,' she reassured him. 'Some Angelspotters see angels when they're still in nappies—the baby Angelspotters I mean, not the angels! Hah, hah!' she laughed. 'And some don't until they've got all their second teeth. There's no telling when.'

Annabelle was quite sure that Piccolo was an Angelspotter. He was immune to Mystification. Annabelle had a special spray which she used to Mystify folk who had seen angel activity. The spray put them to sleep and erased recent memories. It had worked on Henry their paper boy and Kevin the fruit delivery man very effectively, but even a treble strength brew had no effect on Piccolo at all.

'Which can only mean that you're an Angel-spotter, my darling,' Annabelle had told him.

Piccolo sat back down and looked blankly at his list of one, and found himself wondering if there were baby angels, and where they came from.

Outside there was the distant clonk of a cow bell.

'That's the gate,' said Piccolo. 'I'll see who it is.'

Piccolo stood on his front steps and watched as a tiny van—green, red, and white—crunched along the gravel driveway. 'Paulo's Perfect Pizzas' it read on the side.

They must have the wrong address, thought Piccolo, until the driver hopped out. It was Mr Purvis, the dreaded Inspector himself, thinly disguised as a pizza delivery man.

Striding smartly up to the steps, carrying a fragrant box, he said, 'Order for Miss Grande?' Piccolo struggled to pretend not to recognize him.

'Um, Miss Annabelle Grande? This is Holywell, 9 Pleasant Crescent . . .'

'That's right. ExtraLargeFamilyPanfried-VegetarianTriplePineappleNoGarlic. I'm Paulo by the way.'

They shook hands awkwardly, and Piccolo led him inside.

'Your pizza is here, Auntie,' said Piccolo with a tiny shrug. Annabelle looked up from her list-making, then leapt to attention, as if this was a visit from the queen. Even Annabelle, who was not always observant, recognized that this was not a regular pizza man.

'Oh . . . at last . . . mmmm . . . yum. Ah, Piccolo, be a dear and get my purse, which is somewhere . . .' she waved a vague wide circle '. . . you'll find it.'

Piccolo left the kitchen to find the purse,

which he happened to know was in Annabelle's pocket. Two steps beyond the door he stopped to listen. This was poor manners, he knew. His dear missing parents had not brought him up to be an eavesdropper. But these were unusual times. He needed to be alert, but not alarmed.

The Inspector spoke in an annoyingly low drone. Piccolo missed a lot of what he said.

'It's me . . . your Inspector . . . pizza . . . now.'

'Oh, really! Excellent disg—' began Annabelle brightly.

'Shh! . . . the boy . . .' hissed the Inspector.

'It's all right. He'll be gone for hours,' whispered Annabelle loudly, pulling her purse from her pocket with a big wink.

'Good . . . I have to warn you . . . I'll be gone for . . . information gathered . . . remember those cactus robbers . . .'

Piccolo moved half a step closer to the door-way. A floorboard squeaked alarmingly. The Inspector paused.

'Mice,' said Annabelle quickly, and pointing to the pizza she asked, 'Can we be eating this while you talk?'

'What? Oh, yes. As I was saying, there is an angel, recently fallen—an A–RF as we call them—on the loose and somewhere in this vicinity. I will be away to help in the hunt.'

'Now, that *is* a shame. You will miss our party.'

'Party? This is serious, Annabelle. An A–RF can be very dangerous. They are almost demons. So keep your eyes open.'

Piccolo heard a chair scrape.

'Must get going,' said the Inspector, as Piccolo leapt halfway up the stairs then ran down again.

'I can't find your purse anywhere, Auntie,' he puffed.

'Oh, blast my leaking brain! It was here all the time! Bless me much or there'll be trouble.'

The Inspector stood, waiting. 'That will be fifteen dollars sixty,' he said eventually.

'Huh? Oh—you want money! Of course!'

Annabelle counted it out.

When he had safely driven away they sat back down to the list-making, and eating.

'So, you heard all that? You *must* be careful, Piccolo. I could see your shadow plain as purple daylight. If the Inspector catches you out, it will be off to Angelspotter School in a flash.'

'Could that be any worse than a party?' Piccolo wondered ruefully.

Annabelle had made Angelspotter School sound strict and humourless and rigid, but Piccolo wondered if a bit of order and discipline might be a holiday after living with his guardian angel. He looked at her. She was eating pizza with one hand and scribbling down names furiously with the other. Black ink was spraying everywhere.

Piccolo sighed and looked at his list.

'Stella McKellar?' it still read. He ate some pizza, sharpened his sharp pencil and wondered if he should have more friends.

Twenty pages later, Annabelle's list of guests was complete.

'A theme! Now we have to choose a theme!' she cried, bouncing with excitement. 'Everyone has to dress up. How about French Royalty, from the eighteenth century? With those beautiful big dresses, those huge hairdos . . .' sighed Annabelle.

But Piccolo was a practical boy and this sounded too difficult. He suggested a letter theme, 'Pee', for example.

'"Pee" Yes! "Pee" for "Princess Primrose of Provence"—that's a place in France. That will be me! I used to be French, a long time ago. You could be Pinocchio!'

'Um, that's a good idea,' lied Piccolo, and he felt his nose to see if it was stretching.

The Party People had provided bright, amusing invitations. All Annabelle and Piccolo had to do was fill in the details and address the envelopes. And they needed to choose a date.

Annabelle suggested the day after tomorrow, but Piccolo thought that was too soon and suggested a Saturday morning some time in 2022.

'Don't be such a gloomy tomb!' said Annabelle, poking him in the tummy with her quill. 'You'll have a wonderful time.'

They compromised, and chose Saturday the eighth of May.

Piccolo hand-lettered the invitations and typed on the envelopes, while Annabelle folded, licked, and stamped.

The next morning, over breakfast, Annabelle was still remembering important people and scribbling more invitations. Piccolo put the envelopes in his schoolbag. They weighed a tonne. He walked to the letterbox at the end of Pleasant Crescent and stood before it with the great wads of envelopes in his hand, hesitating. There was a stormwater drain nearby. It beckoned him.

'Save yourself the bother,' it said in a deep

hollow voice. 'This party will only bring trouble. Post them in meeeeee!'

Yes. They could all get lost in the mail, Piccolo thought, agreeing with the drain's point of view. Then he felt the prickly neck feeling. He looked quickly around for bushy eyebrows. Mrs Jolly across the road was watering her driveway and gazing at him intently. A very curious lady, was Mrs Jolly. Piccolo quickly stuffed the wads into the letterbox. The drain had lost the argument, thanks to Mrs Jolly.

The party was on.

On the far side of a hedge, on a high ladder, clipping a bush, stood a gardener—with long hairy arms and bushy black eyebrows. He stopped clipping and watched the boy walking away.

Piccolo still had a handful of invitations to deliver at school. Annabelle had made him try a little harder with his own list. At recess he handed

Mrs Jolly across the road was watering her driveway.

some envelopes out privately to three boys in his class. They seemed quite keen to come. After all, there would be camels and a fire-eater, and professional party food. By lunchtime lots of people Piccolo barely knew were being friendly and attentive, hoping for invitations too.

But there was only one left, and that was for Stella. Brian Pomeroy, a large persuasive lad, nearly got hers. Piccolo gritted his teeth and ignored the pain until Brian became bored and got off him.

The groundsman, Mr Yow, had been scratching himself and hovering about all day again, but Piccolo had been too busy to notice. And he did not notice Mr Yow secretly sniffing, like a beagle, around the bags outside his classroom, finding Piccolo's, carefully drawing out the last invitation, furrowing his eyebrows and slowly reading it, and sliding it back in again.

At last, when the bell had rung and school was over, Piccolo screwed up all his courage and walked sideways up to Stella. Even though they had been at the same school for years they had only really spoken a dozen times. Piccolo had always said interesting things like 'Have you finished your homework yet?' and 'Sure is hot today.'

So it was a brave thing that he did when he poked the envelope at her and said, 'There's going to be a party, if you want to come, at our house. But you don't have to.' His ears burned. She would notice them, and that he could barely speak English.

'I'd love to come,' Stella said straightaway. 'I didn't think I was going to get an invitation.'

'Oh, sorry. I was saving yours until last. Brian Pomeroy sat on me but, well, there it is,' Piccolo explained clumsily.

'Sounds like it will be a great party. I'd love to come, thank you. And I'll meet your lucky aunt.'

'Oh. You know about my aunt? Of course you do. She's in the paper a lot. She's very lucky at competitions.' Piccolo's red ears had infected his whole face now. Then he added, 'She's very, um, different though. Very, ah, colourful.'

So, Stella was invited now, and happy to be coming, and she thought she might dress as a periwinkle, if the costume was available. Piccolo said he hadn't decided what he would be yet—maybe a philatelist.

'That's a stamp collector,' he explained.

'Oooh. Exciting,' said Stella.

Piccolo suspected she was teasing him, and he blushed an extra bright shade of crimson.

CHAPTER THREE
The Party, Part One

Saturday the eighth day of May approached rapidly. Answers to invitations overflowed from the letterbox. Annabelle had the best time of her very long life, she said, sitting on the ballroom floor opening them. Piccolo made a list with 'accept' and 'decline' columns. Most of the replies read 'Can't wait!' or 'I'll be there with bells on!'

The Prime Minister was regretful to have to decline, but the bus stop dog would be coming. Piccolo had found his reply, a small bone, on the doorstep. Annabelle could read the chew marks, she said.

Strange replies were arriving too. A woman from *Worldly Women* magazine was coming, as was a man from Brazilian Lotteries.

'Annabelle, I think you've been putting invitations into competition envelopes. Did you really mean to invite Mrs and Mr Browne of Browne's Traditional Custard?'

'Not exactly, but the more the merrier!' she declared.

Piccolo gloomily added a column to his list: 'Coming accidentally'.

Apart from the Prime Minister, every single one of the replies was positive. Piccolo's 'accept' column was far too long. It had spilt off the bottom of the page and on to another, and there were already thirty-two 'coming accidentally'.

He imagined serious overcrowding and mayhem ahead. Annabelle could see only merriment and joy.

'This is a lot of people already. Where's everyone going to fit? And what if it rains? I don't want them inside the house, or in the back gardens.'

'Really, Piccolo, you can be such a worrywart. Everything will be wonderful, and I have some friends in high places who will see to the weather.'

On the Friday the Party People arrived, wearing snappy bright uniforms. They began to assemble, prepare, hoist, pitch, cordon, and trim all about the place. They hung, strung, and beautified in a quiet and orderly fashion. Piccolo was very impressed. Nothing warmed his heart more than watching crisp efficiency, except a long and tidy list, perhaps. The camels seemed very well-mannered. If they had to spit, they spat politely, and never at humans. The donkey, Hortense, was courteous and well-groomed. The fire-juggling rehearsal had him a little concerned at first, but he was amazed by the juggler's precision and skill. Piccolo began to relax a little, and even enjoyed himself trying on different costumes. There was no costume for a philatelist, so he tried dressing as a plumber and a pie man. Eventually, daringly, he settled on being a pirate. Annabelle, dizzy with bliss, was a palomino horse, a pope, and a poodle before she returned to her first choice. She became a princess, French, from the seventeenth century, with hair piled a metre high and a ballooning beribboned dress.

Piccolo toured the preparations in his big boots, sword, and hat. Busy Party People paused to smile and congratulate him on his choice.

'Everything will be all right, Piccolo,' he re-assured himself. He imagined quietly slipping away from the hubbub with Stella, on Abdul the camel, for a tour of the back gardens. He might even show her the perch pond, his special place—although the camel would have to be tied up somewhere—in case he strayed and ate the oranges in the orchard. Anyway, it seemed to Piccolo that Saturday the eighth might be a very good day after all.

The day of the party dawned clear and mild, as Annabelle had promised. The Party People returned early to finish the preparations. Trestles were set under the olive trees with all kinds of fancy fruits and sweet pastries and great glass jugs of watermelon juice. Music murmured sweetly from the wandering players as they practised. The driveway fountain, strewn with floating gardenias, tinkled prettily. Hortense the donkey was dressed in her finest straw hat, and wore a little lipstick. Piccolo wished his dear missing parents could be here to see their home looking so magnificent. Time quickly slipped by. At nine-thirty Piccolo dressed in his pirate costume. At nine forty-five he was struggling to set Annabelle's tower of hair straight. At five to ten—five minutes early, noted Piccolo—the first footsteps were heard crunching down the gravel driveway. People were arriving, their heads swivelling this way and that.

'Will you look at this place!'

The day of the party dawned clear and mild.

'Is that gold plating on that fountain?!'

'Oh, everything is so beautiful!'

The trickle of guests became a flood. Annabelle was flipping and flapping about, meeting and greeting. Piccolo was afraid that her enormous wobbling wig would fall off, or worse, that her angel wings would pop out from under her gown. Suddenly he had an overwhelming desire to run and hide. He felt idiotic standing there with his plastic sword, rubber parrot, and huge boots. But he clung to his post by the costume tent, ushering people inside. The three boys from school arrived together. They admired Piccolo's costume and all said they wanted to be pirates as well. Then Brian Pomeroy appeared, sneering. He had most definitely invited himself. Piccolo would have liked to run him through with his plastic sword, but invited guests began emerging from the costume tent. A postman came out to join the party, then a policeman, followed by two popes and a psychiatrist. His school friends came out as a posse, in fine cowboy style, and ran off whooping. Piccolo began to feel less silly. Mad Mrs Lin arrived, pushing her shopping trolley, but she refused to wear a costume and would not be parted from her trolley, which was rumoured to contain six million dollars. Annabelle had made some interesting friends, thought Piccolo.

Everywhere people smiled and chatted as they nibbled on dainties and sipped sparkling juices. Balloons were twisted into sausage dogs and interesting grubs. Piccolo heard people saying, 'This is the best party since Clearwater Bay survived the cyclone of '74' and other complimentary things. The boys from school, full of cake and excitement, grabbed Piccolo.

'This is the best party since parties were invented!' they yelled, running off to throw water bombs at the mayor, who was dressed as a pickpocket. Even Brian Pomeroy, in the form of a prize-fighter, grunted positively at Piccolo.

If there were any angels in the happy throng,

Piccolo could not spot them. He was too busy to be looking for people with golden glows.

Suddenly Stella was standing in front of him. 'You're here!' he yelped. 'You came!'

'I am! I did!' she smiled. 'You're a good pirate. Do you want to help me choose a costume?'

Piccolo thought he might, so he led her into the tent.

Outside, the party paused to wonder at a magnificent long limousine, gleaming dark silver, moving slowly down the driveway. It stopped by the fountain. A squat, long-armed driver hopped out and waddled around to a rear door. He opened it with a low bow. A tall elegant woman dressed tightly in silver stepped out, her long flaxen hair shimmering softly and her silken cape undulating in the breeze. She was stunning, and there was much staring and many soft 'ooohs'.

'Hello, everyone,' she breathed. 'Can someone show me where I might find a costume?'

Piccolo was struggling with a possum suit. Stella was half inside it, but there was a problem with fur stuck in the zip. The costume tent flap stirred with a breeze smelling of jasmine and newly mown grass. A voice, warm and sweet, asked, 'Piccolo Grande, I presume?'

The boy turned to face the most glorious creature he had ever seen. Leaving the half-dressed marsupial, he lurched forward in his big boots, the rubber parrot bobbing on his shoulder, the plastic sword caught between his legs. The woman smiled and curtsied, as if she was meeting the president of a rich and powerful pirate nation instead of a stumbling boy.

'Hello. I am Elspeth. You must be Master Piccolo. Enchanted.'

She held out her hand. It was Piccolo who was enchanted. He gazed stupidly at the offered hand. What a stunning hand it was.

'Are you busy? Could you help me choose something to wear?' she sang.

Piccolo reached blindly into a rack and pulled something out.

'A pigeon, Piccolo?' She laughed like a tinkling stream. 'A lovely idea, but I think this will do nicely.' She chose a simple diamond tiara from a shelf, put it on and looked a hundred times the princess that his guardian angel did.

'I am an old friend of Annabelle's. Perhaps you could help me find her?' Elspeth asked.

'Annabelle?' murmured Piccolo.

Just as he was wondering if he knew anyone with that name, a raucous laugh from outside jolted his memory.

Elspeth took his hand and led him out of the tent. A grumpy half-possum stood abandoned.

The party guests parted before them. Elspeth glided and Piccolo stumbled towards the rasping laugh.

They found Annabelle in the Feats of Strength pavilion, sweating, grunting, and guffawing as she tried to tear a telephone book in half.

'Annabelle,' said Elspeth, simply and sweetly.

Annabelle swung round as if she had been slapped, spitting hair out of her mouth. She wiped her sweaty forehead, smearing her princess make-up. A button popped off her gown.

At last she said, simply, sourly, 'Elspeth.'

'I heard you were having a party. I hope you don't mind my inviting myself,' Elspeth crooned. Piccolo thought it was a calamity and a disaster that they had forgotten to include Elspeth on their stupid invitation list. Annabelle struggled to make a thin smile.

'Well, here you are . . .' She fidgeted with her messy costume. A bow unravelled. 'You've met my great-nephew, Piccolo. I'm his great-aunt.'

'That is logical. And what a fine boy he is.' Elspeth smiled angelically.

Piccolo was puzzled. Annabelle obviously knew Elspeth, but she was behaving strangely, almost as if she did not like the glorious newcomer.

'Now, would you like to show me about your lovely place, Piccolo?' she sang.

She turned gracefully and glided out of the pavilion, and, smitten, Piccolo clumped along behind. Annabelle watched, dark and scowling, as they disappeared into the crowd. She picked up the telephone book, snarled, and ripped it in half with a single wrench.

CHAPTER FOUR
The Party, Part Two –
the Disastrous Part

Piccolo drifted happily along holding Elspeth's hand. She graciously admired the pavilions and the party hats, the streamers and lanterns. She stepped lightly over squashed pies and burst balloons and camel droppings. Gradually they moved away from the party into the back gardens.

'Ah, it's so peaceful here!' she sighed. 'The party is a little too boisterous for me, I confess. I do so love peace and solitude.' Piccolo was delighted. So did he! He wanted to show her everything.

First they visited the vegetable garden. Piccolo

was very proud of his runner beans.

'Oh, Piccolo! What fecundity and abundance! You grew all this? And look at those runner beans!' The young gardener beamed with pride. Elspeth admired the swimming pool and the diving pool, showed great interest in the birdbaths and birdhouses and sundial and rock wall and statues. It was a thorough tour. They even paid a visit to his old playhouse in the big red gum tree. He laughed as Elspeth climbed the ladder and sat on the playhouse's deck, her legs dangling.

'Ah, what a view. I can see Clearwater Bay from here,' she exclaimed happily.

Later they sat on the swings, swinging gently.

'This is a magical place, Piccolo. You must be very happy here. Although I know you miss your parents, poor boy,' she said gently, touching his arm. Piccolo was immediately overcome with sadness, and missed his dear parents more terribly than ever before.

'But you have been so brave and capable to go on living here alone,' she continued, and Piccolo swelled with pride at his own bravery and organization. It seemed that Elspeth knew everything about him; that she could see inside his soul.

'Tell me,' she asked, 'how are you getting along with your great-aunt?'

Piccolo thought for a moment. 'Ah, well, we are different sorts of people. She's very . . . she's got lots of . . . my aunt is a bit unusual.'

His beautiful guest laughed.

'You are a gentleman, Piccolo! Unusual indeed! Yes, she was always a handful—a noisy, energetic thing she was.' Piccolo had to agree. Elspeth looked around the garden. 'Such a beautiful garden. So many pretty nooks and crannies. Have we seen everything?'

They had: everything except for the compost heap, and one last special place. They had not been to Piccolo's perch pond. Leaving the swings, they passed through the orange orchard, towards the bower of lillypilly trees. Just beyond was the pond. Only his parents and Annabelle had ever been there. Piccolo wondered if he should show his lovely guest. After all, he had only known her for thirty-seven minutes. On the other hand, he had never met anybody so gracious, or so elegant, or so unlike Annabelle. The lillypilly bower stood right before them.

'Ooh, we haven't seen in there,' said Elspeth. 'Can we have a . . . ?'

'Grooooaawll!' Suddenly a great hairy beast appeared and pushed between them. It was Abdul the camel, carrying a large grumpy possum. Abdul growled again, spat accurately at Elspeth's tiara, and snorted on his way. Piccolo, horrified, watched Elspeth's face darken with anger and disgust. She flung the soggy tiara away with a hiss and quickly tried to compose herself.

'Oh. Ha ha!' she said with a brittle laugh. 'I suppose camels must express themselves too!

Suddenly a great hairy beast appeared.

Now, where were we before we were so wetly interrupted?'

Piccolo looked quickly through the lillypilly bower. He decided to save the perch pond for later. As rude as Abdul's interruption had been, Piccolo was surprised and a little shocked by Elspeth's anger.

'Um, do you want to see inside the house?' he asked.

'That would be wonderful too,' his guest said brightly. 'Oh look! Here is your aunt.'

Annabelle stood squarely before them, like an overdressed boulder, blocking the path. Her head and tower of hair were lowered, and her fists were on her hips. She breathed in little snorts like a bull.

'Piccolo. You are needed at the party. Come.' Without looking at Elspeth she stomped forward and grabbed his arm. The boy was marched roughly back to the house.

Elspeth watched them go, and smiled to herself.

Piccolo was angry and alarmed. He had never seen Annabelle like this.

'You're breaking my arm off!' he complained. 'Let me go!'

'Never, ever, trust that . . . that . . . person!' grunted Annabelle as she dragged poor Piccolo along, stumping through dropped buns and donkey droppings. 'She is only here to ruin everything. The party, me, us . . .'

Annabelle stumped through the middle of the fire-juggling act, and stumped on unaware that her tower of hair had brushed a burning baton and was now ablaze.

'Annabelle. Your hair!' cried Piccolo, struggling to get free.

But she was deafened by her fury.

'She is Bad in a tight frock, that Elspeth,' she snarled unangelically and pulled Piccolo along, protesting. They passed under a floating pack of sausage dog balloons and several were lit by Annabelle's towering inferno. The pack floated away, exploding, and ignited a pack of caterpillar balloons which in turn lit the flock of duck balloons. The result was a spectacular showering of little molten balloon fires, falling on tents and decorations and guests. The pleasant party fell rapidly into chaos and pandemonium. A Party Person ran after Annabelle with an extinguisher and put her out. He sat her down, covered in foam, under an olive tree then ran off to fight other fires. People trampled each other trying to escape the flames. A pope tripped and startled Hortense the donkey, who galloped about with a small postman on her back, turning over flaming tables and unhitching tents. The grumpy possum was singed. A prize-fighter fell flat on his wide face. The bus stop dog ran about yapping, trying to round up the camels. Piccolo spun around on the spot not knowing what to do. A siren approached in the distance. Everywhere he looked a small disaster was unfolding. He felt like a small child in a stupid suit, which indeed he was.

Out of the madness, like a shower of cool rain, glided Elspeth, unhurried and serene. Smiling divinely she took Piccolo's hand.

'Shall we sail to calmer waters, dear boy? I'm sure everything is under control.'

The chaos all around them looked completely out of control. Annabelle had ruined everything, Piccolo thought bitterly. If his house burned down it would be her fault.

'Let's go,' he said.

'Excellent,' laughed Elspeth, and she led him away, between burning trestles and over collapsed tents, past distressed overdressed guests and a busy fire engine. Parked on the grass was a long limousine. The driver opened the door. Elspeth sat in the back seat and Piccolo slid in beside her. He looked back at the disastrous party. His gaze rested for a moment on a smoking possum.

'Don't worry, dear. Let me take you away from your troubles,' Elspeth crooned soothingly. Then she laughed again. 'That was quite a show!'

Piccolo slumped back into the rich leather seat and sighed. The great car moved along the drive and turned on to Pleasant Crescent. Mrs Jolly, who had not been invited, scowled at them.

The limousine hummed as they drove along. The warm afternoon sun shone through the tinted windows. After a while Elspeth murmured, 'Would you like to visit my place? I have a small yacht. You will like it, I'm sure, my handsome pirate.'

Piccolo nodded, sleepy in the sun. The rubber parrot on his shoulder nodded too.

CHAPTER FIVE
Piccolo Enchanted

Elspeth's house was built right on the edge of Clearwater Bay. It was open and airy and delightful. Water lapped beneath its wide verandah. There were ferns and potted palms and many happy peach-faced lovebirds in a big aviary. Piccolo saw the 'small yacht' tied up to a jetty. It was long and gleaming white with brass fittings. Elspeth gave him some new clothes and showed him into a bedroom to change. Off came the silly hat, the plastic sword, the ridiculous parrot, and the huge boots. He felt as if he was shedding a skin and leaving an old life behind.

'Welcome aboard,' smiled Elspeth from the stern of the beautiful boat.

Piccolo drifted up the gangplank and joined her. The long-armed driver had transformed into the ship's captain. He waddled about briskly, raising flags, starting the motor, and casting off. Piccolo sat in a deckchair, feeling like a prince on a throne. A matching pair of silent servants brought them tea on silver trays. They were dressed in crisp white and had the same squat build as their captain. The great boat motored softly away from the jetty. Piccolo looked back at the blue hills in the distance, at Elspeth's handsome house and glimpses of the town through the pine trees.

Sunlight danced on the little waves and gulls wheeled joyfully overhead. Something caught his eye in a boathouse near the jetty. Two figures had appeared in a window, waving energetically.

'Who are those people waving?' asked Piccolo, waving back.

'Oh, they are the boathouse staff. Lovely folk.' Elspeth took him firmly by the hand and murmured, 'Come sit with me by the bow.' As he was being led away Piccolo caught a glimpse of hairy arms pulling the wavers away from their window. Everywhere he went lately there seemed to be hairy arms, Piccolo thought.

'Elspeth, are all your, um, servants related?' he asked. Elspeth laughed.

'Yes, you could say that. Now watch your step, my dear,' she cautioned as the boat rolled a little. Piccolo was untroubled by the motion of the waves. He had spent many happy days with his dear missing parents on their yacht, the *Leaping Susan*.

Those were distant memories now, like the memories of another boy.

Some way out into the bay the motors were cut and the mainsail hoisted. Piccolo sat with his back against the main mast, listening to the flap of the sails and the lapping of the waves. Elspeth sat near the bow. A silent servant, who reminded Piccolo of the new school-crossing lady, brought her a small harp. Elspeth stroked the instrument with long delicate fingers. The breeze played with her golden hair as she sang. Piccolo turned his face to the sun. The music swept him away, his heart floating with happiness.

She must be an angel, thought Piccolo, a real one, and he frowned at the memory of his own angel, plunking on a banjo with silly fat fingers and eating bananas. He let the memory go and let the beauty wash over him.

Half a dream later, the yacht anchored by an islet on the outer edge of the bay.

'Would you like to come for a swim, Piccolo?' Elspeth was asking him. On an average day he was not pleased to be in deep salt water. Big toothy things lived down there. But this warm afternoon Piccolo did not feel like his average self. So a new fearless boy dived after Elspeth into the turquoise waters. Brilliant corals greeted them, and soft seaweeds waved. Vivid rainbow fish stroked his face as they swam by. Elspeth collected shells for him and, taking his hand, led him to a cave full of sparkling silver fishes. In a single breath, it seemed Piccolo had discovered a whole new world.

On board again, Piccolo's heart brimmed with wonder. They dried off in the sunshine and the servants brought more refreshments. Piccolo sipped a fragrant tea and nibbled on vanilla wafers. His hostess talked amusingly about many things, but Piccolo was not really listening. Her voice and laughter were a song. The late sunlight gilded her hair.

The boy happily slid into dreams.

Piccolo stirred to find himself in the limousine.

'Ah, you're awake. We nearly have you home. Did you enjoy yourself today?'

He nodded dreamily.

'If you ever feel like a change of scenery, and some different company, you can stay with me on the bay,' Elspeth crooned.

The limousine turned into Pleasant Crescent. Piccolo wondered if his house had been burned down by the party. He might need a place to stay. The great car glided silently to rest.

'Ah, here we are,' said Elspeth. 'I know! Why don't I pick you up in the morning? I have a little seaplane, and we could fly about a bit. What do you say?'

Piccolo wondered, sleepily, if another excursion might make his angel angry again. But she had ruined the party and handled him roughly.

'That would be wonderful,' he said.

'Oh good,' breathed Elspeth, with a satisfied smile. 'Six o'clock then? Sunrise is so special from the air.'

She kissed him lightly goodbye and left Piccolo at the end of the gravel driveway.

For a long while he wondered what he would find at the other end. Eventually he began to walk. In his hand he noticed a large bag. Pausing, he looked inside. There were neatly folded clothes, a toy sword and a rubber parrot, big boots and a feathered hat.

His home came clearly into view. It seemed to

be in mint condition, untouched by the flaming party. Packing cases marked 'Party People' were stacked neatly all about. Garbage bins were lined up at attention.

The only thing out of place was a scruffy creature sitting on the front steps under a blackened wig.

Piccolo stopped. The sooty woman spoke.

'She is not what she appears to be,' said Annabelle, her voice tired and hoarse.

'Yes, she is. She is beautiful. She is like an angel, a real one,' said Piccolo defiantly. His own real angel looked as if she had just climbed out of one of the bins.

'As a matter of fact, she *is* an angel. But she's an unhappy, dangerous one,' said Annabelle, 'and she's trying to take you from me.'

'Rubbish,' said Piccolo angrily, throwing down his bag. 'You're just jealous.' He turned away and strode off to the back garden.

A scruffy creature sat on the front steps.

Sitting with his feet in the pond, Piccolo talked to his perch. He told them the whole complicated story of the day. They swam about in polite little circles, listening and nibbling. Their eyes went wide with alarm at the tale of the party disaster, and round with the wonder of Elspeth and her beautiful boat. The adventure underwater had them leaping about with pleasure. Their eyes rolled with surprise when they learned of Annabelle's dislike for Elspeth, and with alarm when Piccolo said, 'I think I might be going on a holiday, just for a while.' Saying it aloud made the idea sound very possible.

'I'll pack in the morning before Elspeth gets here. Too tired now.'

Lying back on the thick grass, he watched the last light fade from the sky, and slipped into a troubled sleep.

Annabelle paced about the empty house. She had changed out of the silly princess costume at last and cleaned herself up. It had been a big, big day and she was exhausted. Her fury with Elspeth had quietened. She was more cross with herself for overreacting, and for setting fire to the party. And she worried about Piccolo out in the chilly night.

He'll be needing a blanket and something to eat, she thought anxiously. But he's under that witch's spell and won't be pleased to see me.

After a while, she gathered her courage and a few things and tiptoed through the garden. She stopped among the bower of lillypilly trees.

'Piccolo,' she whispered, 'I've brought you a blanket.' There was no answer, so she moved a little closer and whispered a little louder.

'Are you there, Piccolo?'

'I'm here,' he called at last, awake now. Annabelle sighed with relief.

'I've brought you a blanket, and hot chocolate and some party leftovers, and a cushion . . .' she said softly, stepping into the moonlight.

Piccolo grunted a thank you as she put the things down.

'Um, can I talk to you for a minute?' asked Annabelle.

The boy said, 'If you have to,' grumpily.

The angel sat on a mossy rock, pale and serious. Piccolo wrapped himself up in the blanket and took the hot chocolate.

'I need to tell you a tale from long ago. It might help you understand me a bit, and Elspeth.'

Piccolo thought he should be too tired and cross to listen, but he was a boy with pastries and hot chocolate, wrapped in a blanket under a moon. He would listen for a while.

Annabelle began her tale.

CHAPTER SIX
Tales of Old

'Dozens of years ago, hundreds probably,' said Annabelle, 'I was the guardian angel, disguised as a nanny, for two special children. All children are special, of course, but these happened to be princesses. I loved them dearly and they loved me. As they grew and flourished I couldn't help thinking I was a jolly good guardian. Then an angel, tall and beautiful and talented, appeared out of nowhere. Elspeth. She was the guardian angel, disguised as a governess, of the head palace gardener's boys. Grubby things they were—Jacques and Pierre, that's right. But she was not happy, in sight of the palace, with silly, dumpy, happy me inside it. She was brimming with envy, so she plotted to get rid of me and to take my place. And now she is *here*, Piccolo, eons later, trying to do exactly the same thing!' Annabelle shook her head in disbelief.

'No she's not. She's not here to take your place. She's just a lady who likes me,' said Piccolo, angry again. 'And she already has a beautiful place on the bay!'

'Well, nevertheless, she has found me somehow, and found me happy with you. I'm afraid she is here simply to spoil everything by stealing your heart away.'

'You don't want me to be happy with anybody but you,' Piccolo protested.

'That just isn't true, Piccolo. Please hear me out. I'll try to explain.

'At first I was a bit under her spell myself. How she could sing! And so impossibly beautiful.

Then I would find her in the palace with my little ones, laughing and telling them tales and inventing splendid games. I became jealous and worried that they would love her more than me. So I tried to outshine Elspeth.'

'That would have been difficult,' said Piccolo unkindly. Annabelle ignored him and went on.

'Elspeth told my princesses about a magical lynx that lived in the forest. This lynx was a wonderful thing to see. It could climb a tree in a single leap and had fur of spun gold, softer than silk. It could tell jokes in five languages! Then she set her trap. "If your nanny loves you she might take you to see it," she said, or some such rubbish. "Alas, I cannot take you, for I am only the governess of a humble gardener's boys." My little ones begged me to take them to the forest. So I did, without permission. I fell straight into Elspeth's trap. I thought we would wander about happily for an hour or two, have a little picnic by a brook, make some daisy chains. It would be our special secret adventure! And if we happened to see a magical lynx, then I would be their hero.

'All we found were tangly bushes and boggy swamps. We were lost within the hour, and spent a wet night huddling in a hole in the ground. This was no way to treat princesses, so the minute we were found I was put in a dungeon. Elspeth got my job, of course.'

'A magical lynx!' snorted Piccolo. 'You believed that?' He liked the part about Annabelle in a hole in the ground.

'I only *half* believed it. There was a lot more magic in the world then. But you're right, it was uncommonly dim of me.'

'But if Elspeth won and got your job, why would she come here to mess things up?' Piccolo asked cleverly.

'Ah, well. After two thousand nights sitting on cold wet stone, the queen gave me a pardon and I was free. Free, but very cross. And the first thing I saw when my eyes adjusted to the light was

Elspeth. She was high on a balcony like the empress of the solar system, standing there in her glittering gown with her arms around my princesses. She waved to me, *at* me, and grinned like a maniac. Then she blew me a kiss and I'm afraid I snapped a little. I flew straight at her throat. It was awful; the princesses screaming, Elspeth biting. I wrestled her over the edge of the balcony. She had to fly to save herself, in front of the whole palace. There was no point either of us staying—we couldn't Mystify everybody—so we just kept flying. She went north and I went south.'

'So Elspeth *does* have a reason to hate you,' admitted Piccolo. 'Where did you go?'

'I gave myself up to my Inspector, and was sent to the jungle. For many, many years I was a guardian angel in warm green places. I was guardian to a tribe of chimpanzees.'

'Blahhgkk!' said Piccolo, choking on his hot chocolate. He wiped his mouth and tried to hide

I wrestled her over the edge.

his smile. This explained so much about Annabelle, like her fondness for tropical fruits and her popularity with the chimpanzees at the zoo.

'I made many good friends in the jungle,' Annabelle went on. 'I enjoyed carrying their babies and even grooming for lice. I'm still a good climber, by the way. But my angel skills got very rusty, as you know.'

Piccolo knew only too well.

'What happened to Elspeth?'

'Well! Imagine my surprise! I was walking along in the jungle one day, minding my own business and three or four baby chimps, when I ran smack bang into guess who! Yep, Elspeth! She had a bunch of very crabby baboons with her.' Annabelle chuckled. Piccolo suddenly thought of Elspeth's servants.

'Oooh, if looks could kill angels, I would have been dead where I stood. She didn't say boo. Just gave me her evilest eye and turned around with her pretty nose in the air. I didn't see her again until the party. As far as I knew, she was still in Africa, bossing her baboons about. Then up she pops here. I wonder when the Authorities let her out?'

Piccolo tried to picture Elspeth looking for lice on a baboon's back.

'When did they let *you* out?' asked Piccolo.

'Just before I met you. I came straight here, fresh from the jungle to you. I was judged fit for the Guardianship of Humans, on a probationary basis, which means I have to keep having Inspections.'

Piccolo peered into his pond and pondered for a while. He wrapped the blanket tightly around himself.

'This is all so hard to believe,' said Piccolo after a long time. 'And if Elspeth is supposed to be an angel, where are her wings?'

'She has them. We all do. Very handy they are, for getting about. Some angels, like her and the Inspector, are better at hiding them than me.

I used to be able to, but I let myself go a bit in the jungle.' She giggled. 'Besides, leaving them out is a bit like wearing no underwear—very refreshing.'

Piccolo slurped hot chocolate to drown out this embarrassing thought.

'I hate to speak ill of anyone, but everything I've said is true,' said Annabelle.

'She's coming for me again tomorrow,' he quietly confessed.

'Well, Piccolo, I won't stand in your way again, but please think about what I've said. And don't

just look at her with your bedazzled eyes. Try to see her with your heart.' His lumpy angel struggled to her feet.

'Are you going to stay here all night? It's a little chilly.'

Piccolo said he would. He had lots to think about.

'I hope you'll be comfortable, dear boy.'

She waddled away, leaving Piccolo to sigh and look up at the worried moon.

CHAPTER SEVEN
Bad First, Then Worse

The first hint of morning arrived, and with it came Elspeth. Piccolo rolled over on the grass wrapped in his blanket. He heard the faint sound of a car pulling up on the driveway. In a rush the whole strange yesterday, happy and horrible, flooded back to him, and with it Annabelle's strange story.

'Not now,' he moaned. 'Too early.' During the long restless night he had decided not to go and stay with Elspeth, but there was still the day's outing to face.

Maybe I'll just hide in here. Pretend I'm asleep, he thought.

The horn on Elspeth's limousine sounded. Piccolo stood, and slowly left the safety of his special place. It seemed a very long walk round to the driveway.

Even in the grey morning the grand car gleamed. Elspeth stood by it, shining like a beacon. Annabelle's long night-time warning vanished from his mind, and most other things too. He was bedazzled all over again.

'My dear Piccolo,' Elspeth laughed merrily, 'have you been camping out?'

He looked at his rumpled clothes—*Elspeth's* rumpled clothes—and grinned foolishly. She gently took a twig from his hair and brushed a crushed pastry from his shirt.

'Am I too early? I thought we would fly to Porpoise Cove and have breakfast there. And you can tell me if you have made a decision about coming to stay at my place,' she added in a whisper with a wink. A rear door was opened. Piccolo looked at the deep leather seats, but he hovered, hesitating.

'That's a very nice car, Elspeth. Is it yours?' said a voice from the front steps.

Elspeth's eyes flashed and her face clouded, but she spoke lightly and politely.

'Good morning, Annabelle. I'll just borrow Piccolo for a while. Lovely party. Splendid fireworks.'

She directed Piccolo to the car.

'He is not yours to borrow, or to steal.' Annabelle's voice was flat and hard. Elspeth ignored her.

'Let's be going, Piccolo. Time and tide waits for no one, dear heart.'

Heart, thought Piccolo. 'See her with your heart.' How do you do that? he wondered. Elspeth pushed him gently towards the car door but he turned and stepped away from her.

'I'm sorry, Elspeth. I, um, didn't sleep well,

and ah . . . sorry,' he mumbled and walked back towards the house.

'You can't win all the time,' called Annabelle.

'I can and I will,' spat Elspeth, striding after the escaping boy. 'Come on, Piccolo. It is time to go,' she said firmly, taking him by both shoulders.

He twisted away, and with his heart he saw her clearly. Beneath the flaxen hair and perfect skin there was ugliness and much pain.

'No, I won't come,' he said firmly. Elspeth stood stunned for a moment, then hissed, 'You WILL come.' She grabbed his arm hard and held a small spray bottle up to his face. She's trying to Mystify me! thought Piccolo, and he lashed out, knocking the bottle from her hand. In that instant Annabelle leapt from the steps and threw herself at her enemy.

'Leave him, witch!' she cried, knocking Elspeth onto the gravel.

She stood over Elspeth and whispered fiercely, 'Take your stupid big car and go back to the jungle!'

The driver ran over and helped his mistress

up, picking bits of gravel off her as if they were lice. Elspeth breathed heavily and climbed into the car.

'Such a feisty aunt you have, Piccolo. We'll meet again soon, dear boy.'

The car swerved off the driveway to run over a flower bed, and again off the other side to knock over a birdbath. It disappeared in an angry shower of gravel.

Piccolo sat heavily on the front step.

'That was awful.'

'*She* is awful. Awesomely awful. That beauty is barely skin deep.'

Inside, Annabelle sat him on the ottoman and made a soothing banana smoothie for breakfast. They watched silly cartoons and noisy advertisements on the television and tried to calm down. But Piccolo could not concentrate.

'Oooh, look, watermelon only 86 cents a kilo at Buy-Plus!' Annabelle loved her watermelon.

At last Piccolo asked, 'Do you think she'll leave us alone now?'

'I hope so. She was always a difficult angel, was Elspeth, but she seems even worse now. Extra mean, with double nasty on top.'

'Maybe she's the A–RF?' wondered Piccolo aloud as he sucked on his smoothie.

'Oh, oh, I hope not. As much as I definitely don't love her, that would be a terrible thing to happen, to lose her goodness altogether . . . But I wonder . . .'

'I feel like a fool,' he mused, crestfallen. 'She seemed so nice, at first.'

'Ah, first impressions! People, and even angels, are not always what they seem,' said Annabelle the Wise. 'For instance, you might have thought I was a noisy ninny, at first . . . ?'

Piccolo sucked on his smoothie straw noisily, and shrugged.

'Elspeth always put a lot of effort into first impressions and her precious appearance;

stroking her hair, polishing her teeth, hiding her wings. Vanity. All that exhausting vanity has probably driven her mad. I'm your more down-to-earth kind of angel,' said Annabelle. She belched, and laughed. 'See? I'll bet Elspeth never burped once in all her elegant miserable life.'

The next morning was Monday. Piccolo dressed for school as usual. Annabelle offered to walk with him. She worried about what Elspeth might do. They walked through the gardens to the back gate.

'No, really. I'll be all right, Annabelle,' Piccolo insisted for the third time. 'I'll stick to the lanes and keep my eyes peeled.'

Piccolo was worried about Elspeth too, but he could not have Annabelle kissing him goodbye at the school gates in front of everybody. A kidnapping would be better than that.

He set off along the back lane, looking forward to a nice dull school Monday, the more ho-hum the better. Lots of ho-hum would be good, after his big, strange weekend. It would be wise to avoid his party friends, he thought, and especially Stella. After he left her in the costume tent he had forgotten all about her. She might be a bit angry.

There was one busy road to cross to reach his school. Piccolo stopped in a crowd of infants' school children waiting at the traffic lights, keeping an eye out for Elspeth's long limousine. The lights were about to change when suddenly there it was, sliding towards him. He stooped low amongst the noisy six year olds until it passed by.

As he went through the school gate, he heard Brian Pomeroy call out, 'Great party, Pickanose!' Gossiping groups gawked and pointed at him as he passed by. It was not going to be a ho-hum Monday after all. Stella scowled at him twice. At recess and lunchtime all the talk was of the party. The few boys who had been there were telling fantastic stories about camels burning to death and a mass poisoning. Piccolo hid in the library and began covering books with plastic. Outside, the eyebrows of Mr Yow passed by, just above the window sill. They stopped. Mr Yow appeared under them, looked directly at Piccolo, and grinned. Piccolo shuddered at the yellow, pointed teeth and the shine in the black, black eyes.

After school Piccolo set off for home at a fast trot, leaving his classmates behind. He could not stand to hear one more ridiculous party story. Before long he felt the familiar prickling sensation up his spine. He spun round. A hundred metres behind, the dark limousine slowed down and pulled over to the side of the road. Piccolo slid into a lane between two shops and hid behind a big metal bin.

Doesn't Elspeth have anything better to do? he thought, frightened and frustrated, crouching in the gloom. I don't need this! I don't want to be stuck behind a bin being stalked by a vengeful angel. I've got a maths test tomorrow!

After ten tense minutes he peeked over the top of the bin, ducking back down as the big car cruised by again. The rest of Piccolo's journey home was long and exhausting, flitting from tree to fence to bush and constantly looking over his shoulder.

'Where have you been?' said Annabelle with relief as Piccolo came in through the back gate. 'I was beginning to think someone had nabbed you after all, hah, hah,' she laughed, trying to disguise her panic.

Piccolo told her about the sinister limo and

his time in the alley. Annabelle insisted that she would see him to school and back tomorrow.

'Could you not kiss me when we get there, though?' he asked.

Annabelle promised that she would not.

The next morning, Piccolo and Annabelle had an uneventful walk down leafy back lanes. Old Rex, the deaf Alsatian, barked at them half-heartedly through a hole in his fence. A magpie swooped. It began to seem silly to think dark forces were out to nab him. As they approached the school gate, Piccolo said, 'Thanks, Anna-belle,' and accelerated—but he was too late.

'Oh sorry!' said Annabelle as Piccolo wiped his face. 'I just can't *not* kiss that serious little face of yours.'

Somewhere inside the school Brian Pomeroy yelled, 'WHOOOO! Who's your *girl* friend, Pickletoe?'

It was another day of ridiculous party stories. They had grown overnight. Apparently his great-aunt was now in jail, and Piccolo had been sent to boarding school, even though he was sitting with his head in a book on the other side of the room. Fortunately it was a short day. School was cancelled after the lunch break due to an unusually sudden and severe outbreak of head lice. Horrified parents hurried to pick up their scratching offspring.

Piccolo wished that lice were his biggest problem. He looked up and down the street for the limousine before setting off home. The ever present Mr Yow was by the fence, grunting into a mobile phone and scratching his head with a long hairy hand.

'Have you got lice?' said someone at Piccolo's elbow. He jumped. It was Stella. 'I'm still cross with you, so you can have some of mine,' she said, whipping off her hat and scratching her head vigorously towards Piccolo. 'Just kidding, about my lice. Not about being cross. I was hot in that possum suit, which I managed to put on by myself, by the way.'

Piccolo mumbled a sorry, and turned a deep pink.

'Your tall girlfriend had you all to herself,' Stella continued, frowning.

Piccolo shuddered. 'Let's not talk about her,' he said, walking faster. He liked Stella a lot, even cross Stella, but it was not a good time to be chatting. 'I wasn't avoiding you. That . . . that . . . woman is a witch or something.'

'Oh, I see. And she put a spell on you. Poor Piccolo. Well, it sure was an *interesting* party. Did you aunt really get the death sentence?' she asked.

'No, and the donkey did *not* set fire to the fire truck either,' said Piccolo.

A car alarm began shrieking nearby. Piccolo jumped again.

Stella looked at him, dumbfounded.

'That's your second jump in two minutes. You're very jumpy. Is everything all right?' Stella asked.

Piccolo said, 'Fine, thank you,' then dropped to the footpath and crouched behind a bus shelter. Stella looked at him, dumbfounded. A dark silver car drove by. The scruffy little dog that lived under the bench scuttled out and stood over Piccolo.

'Oh, how cute,' said Stella, 'and what are you doing down there?'

'Did it see me?' Piccolo hissed.

'You are behaving strangely and asking odd questions,' replied Stella. 'Did what see you?'

'Is it gone?' insisted Piccolo. 'A big silvery car?' He was breathing heavily.

She looked about. 'There's no big car. There is a boy on a skateboard, and a scary yellow bus!' Stella was being far too funny for a cross person. 'What's going on, Piccolo?'

'I have to go home. Sorry. Thank you, um, for everything.' He ran off.

Stella and the little dog watched him go.

'I used to find him a bit dull,' she confided in the bus stop dog, 'but Piccolo Grande is becoming quite interesting.'

The bus stop dog's hairy forehead was furrowed with concern.

CHAPTER EIGHT
Meeting Mr and Mrs Pheeble

The running boy did not get very far. Piccolo stopped in his tracks at the next corner. The limousine had stopped, waiting for an old lady pushing a shopping trolley to cross the road. The limo tooted its horn, long and low, at which the old lady stopped, turned her trolley and crashed it into the car's expensive paintwork.

Good old cranky Mrs Lin, thought Piccolo as he doubled back past the school and ducked into the lane beside Paulo's Perfect Pizza Parlour, hoping to lose the limo.

'I'm hiding in an alley again,' he sighed, and slumped down at the end of a long line of bins. The smell of sour onions and old dough was overwhelming. He peeked round a bin just as a low, squat shape waddled into the alley. Piccolo sank further into the shadows. Mr Yow! he thought. A similar shape joined the first, poking behind bins and lifting lids. 'That's the lollipop lady. They're looking for me!' The two hunters were only metres away. Piccolo leapt out of his hiding place, boxes and dough scattering, and ran for the far end of the alley. But it was blocked by the great grille and headlights of the dark silver limousine. Piccolo spun round. The hunters stood quietly behind him, showing just enough yellow teeth to stop him trying to barge past. His heart pounded as the squat chauffeur opened a door and out stepped Elspeth.

She smiled, and for a flicker of a moment Piccolo was bedazzled again, and felt foolish for fleeing.

'Dear sweet boy. We did not part on good terms the last time we met. I was hoping to catch up with you,' she laughed a tinkling shower and glided towards him, 'to try to make amends. I'd love you to join me, just for tea and a talk on my verandah. Is now a good time perhaps?'

Piccolo felt completely powerless as the tall sleek woman towered over him, and the hairy people scratched and shuffled close behind.

'I really can't, thank you . . . Homework and things, to do, at home . . .'

'Ah yes, your lovely home. Well, that's a shame.' She reached behind her and brought out a small spray bottle. Piccolo had seen it before, on his driveway. He watched as Elspeth's beauty hardened into a mask, cold as Antarctic ice. She sprayed him firmly in the face. Piccolo remembered his training. This was a Mystification. He fell to the ground and pretended to be unconscious.

'Finally!' said Elspeth. 'One less nuisance in the way. Put him in the back, you two.'

Piccolo was hauled and shoved and dumped on the floor in the back of the car. Elspeth sat in the front with the chauffeur.

'Home, Barrimore. Tie him up nice and tight, Prudence, in the boathouse. Then I'll do away with that fat idiot angel once and for all, and Holywell will be mine.'

Piccolo lay on the floor listening and thinking fast. What did she want with his home when she had one already, he wondered, and what does 'do away with' mean? He had to get away and warn Annabelle, and he had to do it now, before he was tied up in the boathouse. But if he moved now, Elspeth would know he was not Mystified—that he was an Angelspotter. But this was a matter of life and death.

Barrimore, the chauffeur, backed the great car out of the alley. There was a loud clattering crash behind them.

'Aagh! What now?!' shouted Elspeth. Mr Yow and Prudence, the lollipop lady, jumped out of the car, and Piccolo saw his chance. He scrambled out into the street and leapt over the shopping trolley. Mr Yow and cranky Mrs Lin were trading blows. Piccolo ran for his life, or Annabelle's life, or both, with Prudence hard at his heels. He raced round a corner and across the street, leaping over the fence of Saint Barnaby's Church. Halfway through the cemetery, a sharp pain in his leg brought him down hard against a gravestone. The little stone cherub on top looked down on him sympathetically. The lollipop lady had sunk her yellowest and sharpest tooth into his calf. The limo pulled up on the street nearby and Piccolo was thrown fiercely into the boot. Screaming Mrs Lin was left in the alley, crammed into her own trolley.

'*Very* interesting!' said Elspeth, leaning over the boy in the boot. Her eyes flashed with dark sparks. 'An Angelspotter! My new friends will be very interested in *you*!' She slammed the boot lid shut on the frightened boy.

Friends? What new friends? he thought. And why would they find me interesting? She knows I'm an Angelspotter . . . The car swerved, and Piccolo gave up wondering as he rolled about the boot.

Piccolo, trussed up and tired, let himself whimper a bit. He *never* whimpered, not since he was five, anyway, and lost at a railway station, and he was glad no one could see him now. His captors had dragged him from the boot and into a boathouse, blindfolded him and tied him to a post.

I've been an idiot, Piccolo thought miserably. I actually believed Elspeth liked me. He snuffled and shook his head in the gloom.

'Have they gone?' said a voice.

Piccolo immediately stopped his whimpering.

'Yes, the hairy ones have, but they've left us a friend,' said another voice.

'He doesn't seem very pleased to see us,' observed the first voice.

'That's probably because of the blindfold,' said the other voice—a man, thought Piccolo.

'Look at all the blood. He's been chewing his own leg off, to escape, I think. Find a handkerchief for him. He's crying.'

'Not crying,' said Piccolo sniffing. Elspeth had locked him up with idiots. 'Can you help me out of these ropes?'

The owners of the voices fumbled lamely with the ropes for a while, then gave up. With a lot of effort one managed to pull off the blindfold.

Piccolo blinked and recognized his cellmates at once. They were the people he had seen waving in a boathouse window.

'Hello. We are the Pheebles, both of us. I'm Martin. That's Marion. Married, no children, rich, recently moved here from Porpoise Cove. Hairy folk have kept us here for years, weeks even. And the witch, she stole our house. And you are?'

'Piccolo, Piccolo Grande. Look, I really need to escape . . .'

'Yes, we'd like that too. They spray us with stuff, you know. It used to knock us out, but now it just makes us woozy,' said the woman called Marion.

'Woozy and a bit silly too,' giggled Martin. 'And hungry. Do you have any food? They don't feed us much.'

Piccolo said that his school lunch was in his bag if they could find it. They found it, but Piccolo was still wearing it, so it was bound as tightly as he was.

Again he tried to get their attention. 'I have

to get out of here. My aunt is in danger. Do you have a knife or something . . . ?'

'Marion had a dangerous Aunt Mildred once, but she . . .'

Outside a sudden commotion erupted—a growling, a thud, two clunks, a squeal, another squeal and some high cursing, several quick scuffles and a shriek—then silence. Piccolo and the Pheebles held their breath. At last a key rattled into a lock and the boathouse door opened slowly. Piccolo blinked into the dazzling light.

'Oh good, you're alive,' said somebody.

'Stella?'

'Yep, and Mrs Lin. I followed the limo. She's outside tidying up. Ooh—blood.'

Stella untied Piccolo efficiently and, after being introduced, found Piccolo's lunch and fed the Pheebles. Mrs Lin stepped inside.

'I fixed her up good, that hairy woman. She'd better wake up before the tide comes in,' she cackled. Spotting Piccolo's injured leg, she bound it with the Pheebles' handkerchief, muttering and squinting all the while. Piccolo hoped the handkerchief was a clean one.

'Thank you, Mrs Lin,' said Piccolo. Then he asked the Pheebles, 'Do you have a bicycle or a scooter I could borrow? I have to get home immediately.'

'Yes of course, hundreds of the things!' cried Mr Pheeble, much revived by Piccolo's banana. 'Follow me, to the garage! Tallyho!'

Piccolo limped after him into a huge garage beside the boathouse, noticing that somewhere he had lost a shoe and a sock.

Mr Pheeble switched on a light.

Two great cars sat in the garage. One looked very familiar—dark silver with recent shopping trolley scratches. Its bonnet was warm.

'Oh dear! The Mercedes is scratched!' wailed Mr Pheeble. 'And that woman has taken the red Rolls! I never liked her, that witch.'

'Yes you did so like the witch. You liked her a LOT,' Mrs Pheeble corrected him.

'Ahem! Only at first, dear. Now, a bicycle thingy . . . Oh, here we are. Just the one left but she looks like a beauty,' said Mr Pheeble, pointing at a strange contraption in a distant corner. This was like no bicycle Piccolo had ever seen, with its three wheels and two seats.

'That's a tandem tricycle,' said Stella.

'It will do,' said Piccolo, climbing on gingerly. 'Thank you, I'll bring it back as soon as I can.'

'I'm coming too,' said Stella, mounting the seat behind him. 'You'd be faster crawling on your own.'

'Stop,' Mrs Pheeble yelled at them. They stopped. 'A young man cannot be seen in public without a shoe! Martin, give him a shoe.' Piccolo accepted the warm shoe, five sizes too large, and put it on. Stella sat behind Piccolo and did most of the work as they creaked out into the street and rattled off through the town.

They creaked out into the street.

Many townsfolk paused to smile and wonder at the strange vehicle and the serious pair pedalling it. One woman, a newspaper reporter, was more than amused, and poked her pointy elbow into the large young man next to her, who quickly snapped a few photographs.

The pair ran to a car with '*Clearwater Klaxon*' emblazoned on the side, got in and started the engine.

CHAPTER NINE
Starring Stella McKellar

The tricyclists frantically squeaked their way to Pleasant Crescent. Piccolo was in agony and blood was running freely from Mrs Lin's bandage into Mr Pheeble's shoe.

'You really must get that looked at properly,' Stella was saying for the fourth time, when Piccolo suddenly jerked the handlebars, steering off the crescent and behind a shrub.

'They're here, parked in the drive!' he whispered breathlessly.

Stella peered through the foliage. Barrimore

was lounging against the rear of a big red car, smoking.

'I'll have to go round the back.' Piccolo wanted to thank Stella properly, but all he could say was, 'Um, thanks for finding me, Stella, and for pedalling. I'm sorry, you know, for the party . . . I'll be all right now.'

'No you won't and forget about the party. I have no idea what's going on but I know you won't be all right. You could die from bleeding for starters—plus, it's an adventure.'

So, abandoning the Pheebles' antique tricycle and bloody shoe, they backtracked to the lane running behind Holywell.

High on a ladder behind a nearby hedge, a squat, hairy gent clipping a tree watched them go. He dropped his shears and clambered down.

Piccolo and Stella reached Holywell's back gate. Keeping low, they ran quickly through the gardens, paused to drop their schoolbags, and crept to the side of the house. Voices could be heard through the ballroom window. Stella followed Piccolo into the fragrant cover of a gardenia bush.

A tall man in a smart black uniform stood with his back to them. He was talking to Annabelle, pale and still on the ottoman, her head bowed.

'She's still OK! But who is that? Where is Elspeth?' puzzled Piccolo.

The uniformed stranger spoke. 'So, for all the reasons I've outlined—your sloppy and flippant attitude, inattention to your guardee, disrespect for fellow angels—the Council of Inspectors has decided that you are to be moved . . .'

'But I can't leave my boy!' wailed Annabelle.

'Please don't interrupt,' interrupted the man snappily. 'The decision is made. You will return to Africa. The child . . .' he paused to look at a notebook '. . . Piccolo Grande, will be assigned another guardian. You have ten minutes to pack your things. A driver will take you to a nearby headland where you will wait until dark, then you will start your flight.'

'This is an Inspector! He's sending her away!' Piccolo gasped.

'An Inspector of what?' whispered Stella. Piccolo started. He had forgotten she was there with him.

'Can I at least say goodbye?' Poor Annabelle was sobbing now.

'Nine minutes to pack your things,' was the Inspector's answer.

Defeated, she struggled, broken-hearted, off the ottoman. The Inspector turned away from Annabelle and towards the spies at the window. Piccolo pulled himself and Stella down deeper into their bush. He could still make out the Inspector's face through the greenery.

'That's odd. He's grinning. What's he so happy about?' Piccolo parted a leaf or two for a better view. There's something familiar about him, thought Piccolo. The eyes . . . that hard smile . . . Piccolo collapsed inside the bush, struck by a sudden recognition.

'That's Elspeth! She's transformed herself! But surely she's not an Inspector?' Piccolo was baffled. 'No! She's *disguised* herself as one! That's totally illegal. She can't send Annabelle away!'

'What's illegal? What's an Inspector? What on the blue planet are you talking about, Piccolo?' asked Stella.

'Oh. Did I say that out loud? I'll tell you later. I have to stop Annabelle from going. Come on.'

They wriggled out of their hiding place. Piccolo ran, doubled over, to the house, with Stella following, and plastered himself against the wall beside the open back door. He heard Annabelle's heavy footsteps trudging up the stairs.

'Can you stay here and be a lookout? Can you whistle?' he asked Stella.

'Not really. I can yodel, though,' she said helpfully.

'Well, will you, um, yodel or something if anyone follows me upstairs?'

Stella whispered that she would, and took Piccolo's position by the door as he tiptoed inside, avoiding squeaky floorboards, and climbed the stairs.

Annabelle snuffled and muttered to herself as she packed. This was impossible. It was not happening.

Had she really been such a poor guardian, she wondered. Why wasn't her own Inspector sending her away? There was something very strange—yet familiar—about the Inspector downstairs. Her jumbled thoughts and hot tears deafened her to a small knock at the door.

Piccolo knocked softly on Annabelle's door twice, and was poised to knock a bit harder when he heard a wobbly, singing noise from the hallway below.

'Is that ... yodelling?' he wondered. A stair creaked. He fled into his mother's study across the hall and slipped behind the door.

'It's time,' said the Inspector's hard voice. 'The car is waiting ...' There was an enormous wet honk as Annabelle blew her nose.

'And please try to comport yourself with dignity,' said the voice, disgusted.

'I'll ... just ... be a ... few moments.' Honk. Piccolo scarcely breathed behind the door.

Downstairs, Stella scarcely breathed inside a large plant pot. Her yodelling had attracted Mr Yow. He was snuffling and sniffing around the back garden. Soon he was joined by a gardener with the same waddling walk. They found a spot on the path. Blood.

Behind the study door, Piccolo banged his head with his hand. 'Think, Piccolo, think. We need help. If only the real Inspector wasn't away. Maybe he's back. What is his name? Pino, Pronto, PAULO!' Without a better plan Piccolo found a phone book, and flipped through it silently.

'Paulo's Perfect Pizzas.' He dialled the number and closed himself and the phone in a closet to muffle his call.

'We're sorry,' said a mechanical voice, 'Paulo's is closed . . .' Piccolo's heart sank '. . . but please leave a message after . . .' click—'Hello. Paulo of Paulo's Perfect Pizzas here. How can I help you?'

'Oh, you're there!'

'Obviously. What can I do for you?' said the humourless Inspector. Piccolo had no idea what to say next, so he ordered a pizza.

'I . . . we . . . my aunt wants a jumbo vegetarian with extra fruit—lots of banana. And hurry. She says it's an emergency!' He gave the address, hung up and exhaled. 'Good thinking, Piccolo. An emergency fruit pizza. Very convincing.'

Carefully, he left the closet and replaced the phone. Something moved by the door. He turned just in time to catch a glimpse of a hairy hand on the door handle. The door closed with a bang and he heard the sharp click of a key in the lock. Piccolo sprinted over and pulled on the handle. Trapped! He ran to the window. Annabelle was dragging her way along the driveway with her two floral bags. He could not wait for Paulo and his pizza. He had to do *something*! There was still time to yell out. Piccolo struggled with the window. This particular one had always been difficult to open. Now it wouldn't budge. The false Inspector followed close behind Annabelle, his hands on his hips.

'Stop!' Piccolo shouted, banging on the glass.

Annabelle was too far away to hear. With a lot of bashing and a big pair of scissors, Piccolo managed to lever the window open enough to squeeze halfway out. The chauffeur had opened the door for Annabelle, putting her bags on the seat.

'Stop, Annabelle! Stop!' Piccolo screamed. His angel was busy blowing her nose and did not hear him. But the phoney Inspector heard. He spun round, made a sharp gesture to someone out of sight and then pointed at Piccolo. The gardener and Mr Yow climbed up a drainpipe with alarming speed and scuttled across the roof. Annabelle was now climbing into the car. Piccolo wriggled his way out, still shouting and waving his arms. The hairy people tried to wrestle him back through the window, but in the scrabbling and grappling they lost their footing. All three slid then plunged squealing and shouting into the garden below. Piccolo staggered to his feet among the ruined daffodils and saw the car move slowly away.

Too late, he thought as strong hairy arms pulled him down.

Stella poked her head out of the pot. The hunters had gone. She thought about staying where she was. It was quite comfortable inside her pot, and strange things were happening outside. She had heard a commotion—snorting and shouting—Piccolo shouting—up above somewhere. She climbed out and set off to see if she could rescue him again.

I'm getting quite good at saving Piccolo, she thought. But it was a complicated scene at the front of the house. There was Annabelle, climbing into the red Rolls Royce, the uniformed man was waving from the driveway, and here was Piccolo, in a crushed flower bed, entangled with hairy people.

Not knowing what else to do, Stella yodelled again, long and loud.

'Is that yodelling?' Piccolo wondered, again.

One of the hairy people got off Piccolo's back and ran away to investigate. With the last of his strength Piccolo pushed upwards, twisted and kicked. His foot hit something solid and breathy. It was Mr Yow, who now struggled for air.

Piccolo scrambled to his feet in time to see Stella sprinting through the olive trees towards the car, with a hairy man galloping after her. Strong arms gripped him from behind.

'Go, Stella, go,' yelled Piccolo.

The treacherous Inspector, very red in the face, waved his arms about frantically, like an octopus cleaning windows.

Stella was running beside the car now, and then she was ahead, and with great courage she leapt out in front of it. The chauffeur, startled, swerved and smashed noisily into the gate post. The stone urn that sat on top fell heavily onto the bonnet.

Pointing towards the house, Stella shouted,
'Piccolo's hurt!'

Annabelle's door flew open and she tumbled out, clutching her bags. Pointing towards the house, Stella shouted, 'Piccolo's hurt, in the daffodils!' Then, astonished, she watched as Annabelle ran a few steps, unfurled a pair of wings, and flew, fast and furious, over the head of the pretend Inspector, straight for Piccolo. With one deft swipe of a floral bag she freed her boy, knocking Mr Yow in a graceful arc into the flower bed.

'That's Elspeth, Annabelle!' Piccolo panted, pointing at the black-suited man. 'The Inspector is Elspeth!'

'What? Are you sure?' Annabelle watched the pseudo-Inspector running towards her, with his hands outstretched like talons, shouting, 'NO, NO, NO! You don't get away!'

The two angels grappled on the gravel driveway. They struggled and fell, tearing hair, punching and biting. The bogus Inspector had a big advantage in height and reach but

Annabelle was built like a brick shed and was filled with indignant rage.

Stella stood and considered what she had just seen. Piccolo's great-aunt had flown, with wings, along the driveway. And now there were two snarling, yellow-toothed, short, hairy people surrounding her. As she looked around for a weapon, the gardener leapt on to her back, and the chauffeur opened the boot of the damaged car.

'Oh no you don't! I'm not going in there!' said Stella and bit hard into a hairy arm. The gardener shrieked. Stella wrenched herself free. A green, red, and white van screeched to a halt at the gate. *Paulo's Perfect Pizzas*, it read. At the same moment, a car stopped across the road. A camera clicked and whirred.

A stout man, dressed in the same colours as his van, leapt out with a box and several sticks of garlic bread. Barrimore and the gardener turned to the new intruder and bared their teeth. The pizza man glared at them through his heavy glasses and advanced, holding one of the breadsticks like a club. The hairy people lost heart, jumped into the red car, and locked themselves in.

'Are you getting this!' asked a thin, pointy voice in the car across the street.

'I don't know what I'm getting,'—click, whirr—'but I'm getting it,' said another voice.

'Where is Miss Grande?' the pizza man asked Stella. 'Urgent delivery!'

'This way,' said Stella. They ran towards the house.

Piccolo circled around the battling angels on the gravel. He had a stick and tried once or twice to poke the fake Inspector, but it was difficult to be accurate. Anyway, Annabelle was on top now, busily banging the handsome head of her enemy into the driveway. Piccolo looked up to see Stella returning, with the pizza man.

'At last!' he said, dropping his pointless stick.

CHAPTER TEN
An Unmasking

Paulo the pizza man put down his box, marched over to the wrestling angels and beat them with a breadstick until they separated. They sat on the driveway panting, smeared in garlic butter.

'Annabelle. Good to see you getting some exercise. Can you introduce me?' he asked.

'Inspector!' she gasped, and spat out some gravel. 'This is Elspeth! Yes, I see you now, Elspeth. Disguised'—gasp—'as an Inspector!'

'Liar!' screamed the impostor. 'I am an Inspector, you ridiculous fool!'

Paulo, the only real Inspector for kilometres,

stared hard into the eyes of the buttery uniformed man before him.

'Ah yes. I believe you are correct, Annabelle. I'm pleased to meet you, Elspeth. We have been looking for you everywhere.' He held out his hand to help her up.

Elspeth was dumb with horror. Suddenly she leapt up and ran down the driveway towards the red car. She had run only three metres when Paulo said 'Revert'. Elspeth stopped dead. The black uniform paled and melted away. In its place was a scruffy, tight silver dress. Elspeth, the heavenly beauty, writhed on the spot, bound by invisible ropes. She spat and seethed.

'She . . . she . . . !' trembling with rage, Elspeth pointed at Annabelle. 'She can't win. She's ridiculous! She was *born* for the jungle! Look at that hair! And . . . and she's hiding an Angelspotter!'

'Quiet,' said the Inspector coldly. Elspeth was instantly silenced. She fell in a defeated heap onto the gravel. A despairing yelp came from the flower bed. Paulo the Inspector walked towards the sound. Something tried desperately to bury itself in dirt and daffodils.

'And who is this?' asked the Inspector. He leant over and picked up an entirely hairy creature by the scruff of its neck. It was a baboon.

'That's Mr Yow, or it was,' said Piccolo. 'He must have changed when you said "Revert".'

The Inspector deposited the whimpering baboon next to Elspeth. 'In that case,' he said, 'we may have two more monkeys in the red car.' He picked up a fresh stick of garlic bread, waved it in the air and said 'Come'. Piccolo heard an engine start, then the soft crunch of gravel as the big car reversed itself along the driveway. It stopped by the fountain. The heavy stone urn rolled off the bonnet with a thud. Inside, two baboons clung to each other on the floor.

'Open,' said the Inspector. The car unlocked and a door opened. 'Annabelle, kindly see Elspeth and her friend into the car. Thank you.'

Annabelle lifted her defeated foe by an arm and, more gently than she would have liked to, pushed her into the car. The baboon jumped in quickly. Annabelle closed the heavy door with a thud.

The Inspector said 'Confine', and the doors locked. 'And so the great Elspeth is captured,' he said quietly.

Turning to poor bloodied Piccolo and bewildered Stella, he asked, 'Are you youngsters hungry after all that excitement? Would you like some pizza?'

Pizza was the furthest thing from their minds. Piccolo would have preferred a bath and a stitch in his leg. Stella badly wanted explanations. But the Inspector was a powerful being, much more so than Piccolo could have imagined, and he wanted them to eat, so they agreed to eat.

'Good.' The Inspector picked up the box. 'I have here my speciality. It's a . . .' He stopped to listen.

Piccolo heard something too. Click whirr click, whisper.

'Goodness, what a day we are having,' said the Inspector grimly, looking about. 'Hello! Can we help you, behind the pine tree?' he boomed. The clicking stopped.

Todd, the photographer from the *Clearwater Klaxon*, stepped sheepishly out from behind the trunk, and had a silent argument with someone who remained out of sight. Eventually Ms Stringer, pointy reporter, stepped out too, wearing a brittle smile.

'Hello, hello! Lovely to be here. We were just passing by,' she lied, 'and thought we'd check up on dear Piccolo. Ooh, that smells delicious!'

'You are very welcome to try some,' said the Inspector. Annabelle quickly cleared the verandah table to make way for the pizza, and casually threw several cushions around on the floor. When they were all assembled Paulo opened the box.

'Take a whiff of this! Beautiful, yes?' They each

sniffed *the* most pungent, *the* smelliest pizza ever made. It was nothing like the vegetarian with extra banana that Piccolo had ordered.

'It's got triple anchovy, quadruple garlic, quintuple chilli, special imported stinky blue cheese . . .' Inspector Paulo was watching them carefully. It dawned on Piccolo that this was a Mystification. His head spun, his eyes watered, and he was only half acting as he slumped into Paulo's arms. He had to be completely convincing. Elspeth had called him an Angelspotter,

angrily and clearly. Annabelle caught Stella on her way down and lowered her onto a sun-lounger. The *Klaxon* people fell onto the floor.

The Inspector spoke softly to Annabelle.

'I assume that Elspeth's accusations were all untrue?' The Inspector looked at Annabelle, and then he turned his heavy gaze on to the Angelspotter in his arms. Piccolo had to work hard to look Mystified.

'Breathe slowly!' he screamed silently to himself. 'And don't sweat, or twitch. What if he tickles me with something?'

But at last the Inspector laid him on a sun-lounger next to Stella and moved away.

'Elspeth would say and do anything to undo me, the poor troubled soul,' Annabelle explained. 'She must have hated me all these years. What will happen to her?'

'I will inform the Inspector General of Guardians of her capture. You may have guessed that she is the A–RF.'

'The Angel—Recently Fallen! I had no idea she would go so bad. How did she get here, and what does she want with Piccolo, and . . .' Annabelle blurted.

'As you know, I am not permitted to discuss this with you . . .'

'Yes, yes I understand, of course,' said Annabelle carefully.

'But,' Paulo continued, 'considering the exceptional circumstances, I feel that you . . .'

'Would you like a cup of tea, Inspector, and some banana cookies?' Annabelle interrupted. And that was all Piccolo heard as they moved inside the house. He lay on the lounger for a full minute, squirming with curiosity. I can't stand this, he thought, and carefully opened an eye. Then he opened the other, lifted his head and looked about. All was quiet. Piccolo slid off the sun-lounger, stepped over the sleeping Todd and snoring Ms Stringer and crept into the hallway. In the kitchen an awful tale was unfolding.

An awful tale was unfolding.

'. . . and she trained her baboons to trap other creatures,' the Inspector was saying. 'Everything from tiny spider monkeys to elephants. For years she sold wildlife to evil traders.'

'No!' gasped Annabelle.

'Yes! And she even sold baboons from *her very own troop*. In the end there was only a handful left. She became hugely rich and she used some of this money to bribe her Inspector into letting her escape.'

'This is shocking!' said Annabelle, her eyes aglow with gossip.

'Shocking and strictly secret,' he reminded her. 'The Authorities have been on her trail ever since she left Africa. I've been away on the hunt until today!' The Inspector shook his head sadly. 'And now it appears Elspeth tried to transform her remaining baboons into humans.'

Annabelle was doubly shocked.

'But only Inspectors and higher ranks can transform animals to humans!'

'Yes, which is why she only half succeeded, poor confused creatures.'

'But did she really come all this way just to spoil things for me?' asked Annabelle. 'That doesn't make sense.'

'No, it doesn't. But we have ways of making her talk . . . nice ways, of course.'

Piccolo wished that he was not an unmystified eavesdropper. He desperately wanted to tell them what Elspeth had said in the car; that she was after Holywell, and that she had 'new friends' who would find an Angelspotter like Piccolo fascinating.

The Inspector made standing-to-go noises. Piccolo scurried back to the verandah. He trod on something as he stepped over Todd. It was a camera, full of curious shots of strange goings-on at Holywell, Pleasant Crescent. Piccolo quickly slid the strap over Todd's big dopey head, and fumbled with the camera, trying to remove the film. Footsteps echoed in the hall. There was no time. He kicked the camera under his lounger, flopped down and tried to appear deeply asleep. Annabelle and the Inspector stepped on to the verandah. Sweat trickled down the boy's face.

The two angels noticed nothing unusual. They were busy dragging the newspaper folk to the car and heaving them into the boot.

'Keep an eye on those children,' said the Inspector. 'I gave them a strong dose. They saw far too much angel business today. If symptoms persist, call me.'

Annabelle nodded very intently.

'I will now unload this car-load of sorry passengers, deal with the *Klaxon* car, and return for my van,' he said, pausing to breathe. 'You will have to get the girl home somehow and I saw an antique tricycle on the street. I assume it is mixed up in this messy business somehow, so that's your problem too.' He looked at Annabelle for a long moment. 'Things are never dull around you, are they, Annabelle?' he said wearily.

'Well, no. I mean, sometimes. I mean, I try to do my best,' she smiled sheepishly.

'Um,' the Inspector added, looking a little embarrassed, his moustache twitching, 'I will have to ask you to pay for this pizza, too. It's the budget cuts, you see. Things are very tight.'

'Oh,' said Annabelle, 'I'll fetch my purse.'

'It comes to $19.50, including the garlic bread,' he called after her awkwardly.

Lying silent and still on the couch, Piccolo thought indignantly, But it wasn't what I ordered, and it's horrible.

CHAPTER ELEVEN
Pizza by the Pond

Stella smiled as she lay on the grass. 'Mmmmm. That was my first fruit pizza. Surprisingly good,' she sighed. 'But I've eaten too much.'

'*Burp!* Me too!' agreed Piccolo. 'Excuse me.'

Annabelle had set out a little picnic on the grass by the perch pond, and all three had eaten just one slice too many, as is the way with pizzas.

'It's the double banana that really fills you up,' she laughed. They lay contentedly looking up through the leaves, listening to their busy tummies and enjoying their turn when the perch nibbled their toes.

A little later, Annabelle looked over at Stella, who seemed to be dozing.

'That was so clever, how you fetched the Insp . . . Paulo,' she said to Piccolo quietly. '*And* how you saw through Elspeth's disguise. She had me completely fooled.' Leaning towards him she whispered, 'You really *are* an Angelspotter, you know.'

'That was mostly guesswork and intuition. I still haven't spotted one properly, you know, with the golden glow,' he said. 'I doubt Elspeth had a golden glow. A sickly browny-green glow, maybe.'

'Who has a browny-green glow? What are you two talking about?' asked Stella sleepily.

'Oh. You're awake, dear?' said Annabelle with a little start. 'I'm just telling Piccolo what a clever and unique boy he is. You agree with that, don't you, Stella?'

Stella said, 'Hmmm, yes, he's a bit of a genius I guess.'

Piccolo blushed, of course.

Four days had passed since the driveway war. To celebrate their victory they had been to the zoo, and Piccolo had invited Stella to join them. He was in awe of her courage and very grateful to her for rescuing him. It was also four days since Stella had been Mystified by pizza. She could not remember much about that Tuesday, except something about lice and talking to Piccolo at a bus stop. She had a fuzzy memory of riding a squeaky thingy, and hiding in a pot, but she thought these were bits of dreams. Anyway, she was pleased Piccolo had asked her along. Somehow she knew that he was much more interesting than he looked.

At the zoo, after a quick visit to Piccolo's sleepy favourites, the reptiles, they visited Annabelle's chimpanzees. On their first trip to the zoo, Piccolo had found her chatting to them, in Chimp, loudly. It was terribly embarrassing.

'Do you think you could keep it down a bit today, Annabelle?' he asked on the way to the enclosure. 'And not climb the cage this time?'

'I did get carried away, didn't I?' she grinned. 'I just love them so much!'

'My aunt is a bit of a chimpanzee celebrity,' Piccolo explained to Stella. She was not surprised.

Annabelle was greeted with much excited chattering and whooping.

'OOeeee ough, ough offf,' said Annabelle.

'EEEEEooooh pphhhoogluck?' asked a chimp. Annabelle translated for Piccolo and Stella.

'Bonongo here says "Hello and did you bring any bananas?".'

The talk went on with many OOOs and EEEs.

'Very interesting!' said Annabelle. 'Mary says we should visit the baboons. Apparently there's been a big boobiff, sorry, a big commotion, over there for many sleeps.'

The baboons *did* seem grumpy and depressed.

Squabbles kept breaking out. There were bashings and bitings. Two of them were fighting over a hat—a familiar looking chauffeur's cap. High up on the concrete rocks sat a stately baboon, straight and tall, wearing a shabby dress that might once have been silver. Two others were grooming her as she examined herself in a tin lid. Piccolo and Annabelle looked at each other.

'Elspeth!' they whispered.

'I know that name—I think. Who's Elspeth?' whispered Stella.

The queenly baboon spotted them. She shrieked instructions, waving her elegant hairy arms about violently. A dozen angry baboons began hurling skins and peels and things worse in their direction. They ducked and hopped about until Annabelle caught a pineapple top in her hair, and they agreed it was time to go.

On the way home on the bus, Annabelle had a sudden urge for pizza; a Paulo's Perfect Pizza in particular.

They disembussed and Piccolo and Stella waited at the bus stop while Annabelle crossed the road, still wearing the pineapple top, to order. The little dog that lived under the bench hopped up and sat next to them. Stella scratched its head. Piccolo could see Annabelle chatting away with Inspector Paulo. At last she returned with two fragrant boxes.

'Were you two talking about anything interesting?' Piccolo asked.

'Oh, not really. Just confidential pizza recipes.' She winked broadly, chuckling. The little dog chuckled too. 'Harf, harf, harf.'

'Pizza secrets?' wondered Stella, who had a strong feeling there were other secrets as well.

All the way home Piccolo wriggled with impatient curiosity. He was wishing now that Stella, as much as he admired her, was elsewhere.

Later, by the perch pond, full of fruit pizza, Piccolo said he felt sorry for the baboons at the zoo.

'Not for all of them, you don't,' said Annabelle flatly.

'Well, I wouldn't want to be locked up for ever,' Piccolo insisted. In spite of all that had happened, the sight of Elspeth the baboon in a tattered dress had touched him.

'I agree with you, Piccolo,' agreed Stella sleepily near the tree fern.

'Yes, but you would lock *yourself* up, for ever *and* a day, if you'd done what *one* of those baboons had done,' said Annabelle.

Stella lifted herself up on her elbows, looking a little annoyed.

'Pizza secrets, bad baboons . . . you two are being very mysterious again.'

Annabelle looked at Stella, then at Piccolo, then at the second, unopened pizza box.

'Yes, we are being mystifying, aren't we, Piccolo?' and again she winked boldly. 'Life is a strange and mysterious thing, and some things are better not known.' Annabelle picked up the box. 'Stella, would you like to try some of this one?'

Before Stella could say 'I'm totally full', Annabelle opened the box in front of her face. Even from where he was lying Piccolo's eyes watered.

His poor friend was being Mystified with one of Inspector Paulo's super-pungent, knock-out pizzas. Stella fell flat in a faint. Annabelle watched her for a moment, and poked her gently with a fallen lillypilly branch to be sure she was asleep. 'Good. Now I can tell you firmly and absolutely that I cannot tell you what the Inspector told me. It's confidentially secret, I'm sorry.'

'Ah. So you were talking about Elspeth with the Inspector. I thought so.'

'No. Did I say that? Stop hounding me,' Annabelle pleaded.

'So what was Elspeth really doing here? Did they make her talk? Is she the A–RF? Who turned her into a baboon? Will they ever let her go? She told the Angel Authorities I'm an Angelspotter. Do they believe her?' Piccolo asked rapidly, reading from a mental list.

'Arrrgh, all right! You win, you pain in the wing joint.'

Annabelle told Piccolo everything she knew.

After all, if forbidden secrets are shared they might as well be shared fully.

She told how Elspeth had bought a ship, an old tramp steamer, and sailed away from Africa, and how she had made the money for this by selling wildlife trapped by her own troop of baboons whom she half-transformed, and how she had bribed her Inspector.

'Yes, I know those bits,' interrupted Piccolo.

'How do you know those bits?' Annabelle wanted to know. 'Have you been eavesdropping again?' Piccolo confessed that he had heard a little.

'Humph!' said Annabelle. 'Then you know how she arrived at Clearwater Bay, sneaked about until she found a house she liked, then, bold as brass, walked straight in. It was a one-woman, four-half-baboon home invasion. They locked up the poor Pheebles for weeks. Fancy nearly starving to death in your own luxury boathouse?'

'The Pheebles waved at me when Elspeth

took me out on their yacht. She said they were staff . . . I saw something was strange, but I wasn't thinking clearly that day.'

'No, you were exceptionally dim,' Annabelle had to agree.

'She was very powerful,' Piccolo protested. 'I'm just a small boy, don't forget.'

'I know, I know, poor baby,' Annabelle apologized.

'More secrets, please,' said Piccolo.

Annabelle obliged. On Wednesday night Elspeth had been found guilty by the Grand Council of Inspectors on 217 breaches of the Angel Conduct Code, and was sentenced to be a monkey.

'And when they asked her why she was here in Clearwater Bay, she would only say, "To teach Annabelle a lesson".'

Piccolo thought for a while.

'She definitely wanted our home for some reason. After they caught me, Elspeth said she was going to get rid of you, and Holywell would be hers.' He paused and gathered his thoughts again. 'Then I escaped for a while, so she knew she hadn't Mystified me.'

'What!?' shouted Annabelle, so loudly that Stella stirred a little. 'Why didn't you tell me this! Lordy, lord! She knows you are an Angelspotter!'

'Yes, but it doesn't matter any more, does it? Elspeth will be a baboon for ever, won't she?'

'I hope so, for your sake,' said Annabelle seriously.

'Me too. She had new friends who would *love* to meet me, she said.' Piccolo shuddered. 'Who would they be, Annabelle?'

'Not nice friends, I'm sure. Let's hope we never find out, my love.'

Piccolo lay watching the clouds drift by and wondered about his dear missing parents. Sadly, he wondered what they were doing now. His angel squeezed his hand. His heroine slept softly.

Stella fell flat in a faint.

The perch gently nibbled his toes and he started to doze.

Suddenly Annabelle sat up and said brightly, 'Piccolo! I've got a great idea. Let's banish these gloomy fears and celebrate our victory properly with a big party—a better party! How about a Primate Party? I'll be a gorilla—what will you be? How about a proboscis monkey? You know, the big-nosed ones. Or a lemur. They're cuter.'

She looked over at Piccolo. He was up on one elbow, wide awake and staring at her with disbelief. Was she serious?

'Just kidding!' The angel laughed until tears ran over her round red cheeks.

'I really, *really* hope so,' said Piccolo.

Annabelle chuckled merrily, singing, 'Got you, got you.' The boy smiled grimly. The perch leapt about, their eyes bright with happiness. Stella slumbered peacefully.

THE
END

Dave of the Stinky
Cheese Gypsies

The creepy Mr Tompkins
of the Dependable Bank

COMING SOON . . .

PICCOLO AND ANNABELLE
VOLUME THREE

THE STINKY CHEESE GYPSIES

*In the aftermath of the disastrous party, and all that
followed, Piccolo was looking forward to getting his life
back into some sort of order. That is, were it not for
delivery vans coming and going all day. His fine old
house had become an obstacle course of prizes that
Annabelle had been winning at an alarming rate. And
little did Piccolo know that her latest windfall was
about to lead them into a gangload of trouble . . .*

'Piccolo! Look! I won it!' Annabelle shouted
joyfully. She was riding a motor scooter, with a
sidecar attached, round and round the driveway
fountain. Everything was a startling lolly pink;
scooter, sidecar, and rotund rider. She skidded
to a stop by Piccolo. He stood gaping.

It was crazy and hopeless trying to escape.

'I won it!' Annabelle repeated, beaming. 'Isn't she beautiful? I've called her Pootles and the sidecar is Little Toot. And look!' She spun round on the seat. The back of her jacket read 'Heaven's Angels'.

'But you can't drive. You haven't even got a licence!' said Piccolo at last, exasperated.

'Of course I can drive. I got here, didn't I? Let's go for a ride.'

Piccolo should have said 'No way in the world!' But Annabelle was so excited, and promised never to win anything else ever, and it was only going to be a tiny drive to the end of their ever-so-quiet crescent. Piccolo found himself sitting in Little Toot wearing a polo helmet and swimming goggles to protect his eyes. He felt very silly, and felt that things were slipping out of his control again.

'Are you comfy dear?' shouted Annabelle, a bit deaf inside her helmet. She took Piccolo's stiff silence for a wholehearted 'yes', yelled 'Yeeehah!' and took off down the driveway.

ABOUT STEPHEN AXELSEN

Born in Sydney a long time ago, Stephen has illustrated hundreds of children's stories and cartoon strips since 1974 and this is his fourth book as author and illustrator.

Stephen lives by the beach, watching the tides, near Byron Bay with his wife, Jennifer, and two big children, Lauren and Harlee. They share their house with a dog named Oscar, a cat called Willow, and their budgie, Trippy. When not illustrating or writing, Stephen might be found gardening, walking Oscar, or reading until he falls asleep. He also hunts cane toads on summer nights, but not for pleasure!

ACKNOWLEDGEMENTS

I would like to thank everyone mentioned last time as well as Jessica who knows all manner of things and Nerrilee who once danced on a table.